For Clover Rae, Sophie and Ollie –
with all my love xx – **S.P.**

For Isla, who I'm sure always remembers
to say "Please!" X – **N.R.**

BLOOMSBURY CHILDREN'S BOOKS
Bloomsbury Publishing Plc
50 Bedford Square, London, WC1B 3DP, UK
29 Earlsfort Terrace, Dublin 2, Ireland

BLOOMSBURY, BLOOMSBURY CHILDREN'S BOOKS and the Diana logo
are trademarks of Bloomsbury Publishing Plc

First published in Great Britain 2024 by Bloomsbury Publishing Plc

A catalogue record for this book is available from the British Library

ISBN 978 1 5266 3087 2 (HB)
ISBN 978 1 5266 3086 5 (PB)
ISBN 978 1 5266 3085 8 (eBook)

13 5 7 9 10 8 6 4 2

Printed and bound in China by RR Donnelley Asia Printing Company, Dongguan, Guangdong

MIX
Paper | Supporting
responsible forestry
FSC® C144853

To find out more about our authors and books visit www.bloomsbury.com and sign up for our newsletters

PLEASE!

SiMoN PhiLiP

BLOOMSBURY
CHILDREN'S BOOKS
LONDON OXFORD NEW YORK NEW DELHI SYDNEY

NaThAn ReeD

You might think that **manners** don't matter.
You might find **politeness** a bore.
But after I've told you what happened to Bill,
you'll see they could not matter **more**.

Thank you!

It started when Bill wanted ice cream.
He asked for **six** scoops:

"Give me loads!"

But as he forgetfully didn't say please . . .

...he was **kidnapped**

by **alien** toads.

Bill found himself inside their spaceship;
he learned that they'd travelled from Mars.

And then, on a whim, they'd flown down and picked him
to join in their tour of the stars!

The toads were content, but Bill wasn't.

"I want to see **planets!**"

he said.

But as he forgetfully didn't say please...

...they

crashed

in the

jungle

instead.

Bill took in the
beautiful setting,
but soon he was filled with
dismay,

on catching a glimpse

of the **tigers**

and **chimps**

and **crocs** that were
heading his way...

The helpful crocs soon fixed the spaceship,

and everyone clambered aboard,
excited and keen to see sights they'd not seen
and places they'd never explored.

Then Bill, feeling hungry, suggested
they stop for an afternoon snack.

But as he forgetfully didn't say please . . .

... they were **dropped** right

on top of a **yak!**

Whoop!

Bill grinned as they raced through the **mountains**,

Whoop!

he laughed and he **whooped** and he cheered,

But soon went quite stiff at the edge of a **CLIFF**, which rather too quickly appeared.

"Stop running!"

Bill shouted in terror, and tugged the yak's
reins with his hand.
But as he forgetfully didn't say

please,

it
leapt . . .

...to a **fairy-tale** land.

The yak charged top-speed
at some **witches**,

the toads were attacked
by bold **knights**,

while dragons and lizards
fought **wagons of wizards**,

and **trolls** wielding clubs started fights.

"This madness must finish!"

Bill shouted, evading a club and a curse.

But as he forgetfully didn't say please . . .

...the chaos got weirder and **worse**.

Huge **pumpkins** rained down
from the heavens

and **beagles** blew in
on the b r e e e e e z e,

while **llamas** in coats
tickled **farmers**
in boats,

and **cheese-mongers**
sneezed referees.

And that was when Bill started thinking,
and realised he must be polite.

"I'm sorry!"
he shouted.
"Just stop this now,
PLEASE!"
which …

...quickly

put

everything

right!

The **witches** sent
everyone homeward
(once Bill had said "Bye!" to the croc).

In no time at all, he was back at the stall,
to find it was **ice-cream** o'clock.

And finally, Bill had discovered that **manners** do matter a lot.

MR SIMON'S

So, knowing the worth of that magic word 'please',
he should have said **'thanks'** …

...but forgot!